John Oliver Hobbes

A Bundle of Life

John Oliver Hobbes

A Bundle of Life

ISBN/EAN: 9783337093921

Printed in Europe, USA, Canada, Australia, Japan

Cover: Foto ©Raphael Reischuk / pixelio.de

More available books at **www.hansebooks.com**

A BUNDLE OF LIFE.

Pseudonym Library.

THE

PSEUDONYM LIBRARY.

JOHN OLIVER HOBBES

A BUNDLE OF LIFE

NEW YORK

J. SELWIN TAIT AND SONS

65 FIFTH AVENUE

1894

A BUNDLE OF LIFE

BY

JOHN OLIVER HOBBES

AUTHOR OF " SINNER'S COMEDY," " SOME EMOTIONS
AND A MORAL," " A STUDY IN TEMPTATIONS,"
ETC.

PROLOGUE.

I.

SIR SIDNEY WARCOP was a gentleman who had been born with many good and perfect gifts, but he had pawned them to his Adversary for a few casks of brandy and a little soda. In his early manhood he had been considered a handsome, dashing young buck of the old school, a three-bottle hero, a sad dog, an irresistible rake—a good-hearted devil. Now he was reformed, however, and reformation had meant in his case, as in that of many, the substitution of many disagreeable virtues for a few atoning sins. Once over-generous, he was now frugal; once fearless, he was now discreet; once too loving, he was now indifferent; once a zealot, he was now unprejudiced; once candid, he was now abyssmal—in a phrase, he was the embodiment of gentlemanly correctness, well-bred honor, and polite religion.

At the age of six and twenty he had surprised society in two ways: first, by running away with his enemy's wife; and secondly, by marrying the lady on the death, some months later, of her distracted husband. Eighteen years had now passed and, by living in close retirement, Lady Warcop was become a much-sought-after person. She had suddenly inherited, too, a considerable fortune, and as views on marriage are only immoral (as it would seem) when one cannot afford to pay for them, it was not so much a question whether her ladyship would be received, but whether **she** would receive. And she gave such delicious dinners ! The early transgression of Sir Sidney and his wife was forgotten, and their daughter (whose age was a subject delicately avoided by the feeling and discreet world), was receiving her education in a convent abroad. It is possible that she would have remained there always and ended her life as a nun, but for the great interest most unexpectedly shown in her welfare by **a** rich and childless aunt—her mother's own sister—Mrs. Constance Charlotte Portcullis.

The heart of Mrs. Portcullis was, as it were, a moral scent-sachet, which she refilled with the fashionable perfume **of each** season, scattering the musk of the old year to make room for the myrrh of the new. This custom—which is commonly called Toleration—won for her numberless acquaintances of every rank and opinion, among whom it would it have been hard to decide, which expressed his or her contempt for the lady's uncertain principles, in the most affectionate manner. Mrs. Portcullis had, nevertheless, one fixed and unalterable idea, and that had reference to Lady Warcop. She held that her appalling conduct had brought perpetual disgrace on that distinguished family the Tracy Tottenhams, of which she and her ladyship were members. Years passed and the sisters never met. Mrs. Portcullis, of Belgrave Square, and Lady Warcop, of Curzon Street, were a new heaven and a new earth asunder.

They were brought together at last in a street accident. Mrs. Portcullis was thrown out of her victoria and driven home half insensible in Lady Warcop's brougham, which, by a dispensation of Providence or the interference of Satan, happened to be passing at the time of the catastrophe. On recovery from the shock Charlotte felt constrained to write to her sister in pious and forbearing terms—

"Since the Almighty," she wound up, "has, in accordance with His inscrutable Principles, chosen a weak and sinful agent for the accomplishment of His all-merciful design (the preservation of my life), I must accept this as a sign that He desires me to unbend from my former attitude of just, if reluctant, severity. If He has seen fit to forgive you for the disgrace and reproach you have brought on our once stainless name, my duty as a Christian forbids **me** to make any further comment on your crime. But I cannot refrain from adding that my unceasing prayers for your repentance have **no** doubt furthered, more than it would become **me** to say, this miracle of grace.

" I will receive you this day week between two and four.

" Your affectionate sister,

" C. C. PORTCULLIS."

Like Lady Lurewell in the comedy, Mrs. Portcullis could dress up a sin so religiously that the devil himself would hardly know it of his making. It is certain that she deceived herself, and on reading over the foregoing she almost felt the prick of her immortal wings—which prick, as Plato tells us, is to the soul what the cutting of teeth is to the infant.

But Lady Warcop's state of mind on receiving the letter, and her consequent remarks to the effect that Charlotte always was a hypocrite, a cat, and a fool, need not be insisted on here ; for, remembering Charlotte's wealth and several others matters, she wrote her reply in so meek and quiet a spirit that the hasty utterances of her unconsidering tongue shall not be known till the last Judgment. Although, as we have said, Lady Warcop had gained for herself a certain sneaking acknowledgment from so-called good society, her own sister's refusal to recognise her had always been a stumbling-block. There were still many desirable acquaintances who would not wink until Mrs. Portcullis winked, and this consideration was of such moment to Blanche, who only lived now to meet the right people in the right

way, that rather than miss the
chance of reconciliation with Charlotte, she would have performed
even a more severe penance than
did Henry II. at the shrine of St.
Thomas of Canterbury. So giving
much incidental praise to the
Creator, but much more to Mrs.
Portcullis, she wrote to say that she
would call at Belgrave Square on
the day and between the hours
named in Charlotte's most kind
letter, and, begging her to continue
her fervent supplications to Heaven,
she remained her devoted, if un-
worthy, sister Blanche.   She displayed very correct taste, Charlotte
thought, in omitting the ill-gotten
name of Warcop.

II.

LADY WARCOP was a woman of
medium stature, elegant mould,
and cautious smiles. Deep-set blue

eyes and a very low brow, a nose inclined to the Roman, and a telling mouth; a smooth, rather pale complexion and innocent fair hair were the most remarkable points of a countenance which fascinated reason and looked reproach at distrust. At least seven years younger than Sir Sidney, and of singularly youthful appearance, she affected an artless manner and displayed now that childish merriment not seen in children, and now that rudeness which passes for sincerity and is usually found in the disingenuous. A being with many emotions but no heart, with ideas but no thoughts, there was so little, even in her folly, to excite interest, that, in calling her stupid, **friends said** their best and enemies their worst of her character. But the strong force in Lady Warcop was her sex: weak, untruthful, cowardly, and malicious,

she was still no more than woman
may be, and it was no slight virtue
—though a negative one—to have
kept this feminine quality, to have
retained—after a life of sham passions and passionate shams—that
indefinable Eve-like pathos which
from the beginning conquered —and
until the end will conquer—the rig-
our of strict criticism.

Mrs. Portcullis, on the other hand,
was big-boned, loud-voiced, and
mighty, and so aggressive in her
merits that she would have been
more acceptable and pleasant for
one of Lady Warcop's cowering
faults. Her high, white forehead
and long chin gave her a grand and
monumental air, which her widow's
cap, crape robes, and such-like par-
aphernalia of woe made the more
emphatic.

The meeting between these two
ladies, who had hated each other so

long and so cordially, was of the
most edifying and tender nature.
Blanche, who had intended to be
dignified though pious, fell to **miserable** weeping, and Charlotte,
touched by what she supposed **was**
the sacrifice **of** a contrite heart, pro-
nounced, goddess-like, a solemn
benediction on Blanche's bowed
head. Lady Warcop's tears, however, were those of suppressed rage
and spite, and Charlotte's comfort-
able words, "I will make no reference to the past," sent her into
fresh spasms of grief. She remembered every quarrel of their earliest
childhood : how Charlotte had
always been the "good" one, the
"forgiving" one, **the** one "who
would grow up a comfort to her
parents," the one who conscien-
tiously picked plums out of her cake
because they were bad for her—
which plums, by-the-by, she used

to drop on the plate of the less self-controlled **Blanche**. Not vainly, alas! But then, Charlotte did not like the taste of plums, preferring caraway seeds! The plum story loomed big in Lady Warcop's brain, and she howled—not for her own sins, but at the remembrance of Charlotte's treachery some thirty years before, when they both wore pinafores, and were only learning to be hypocrites. .

"I would not have known you," sobbed her ladyship, "how you have changed! What trouble you must have had! Oh, Charlotte! **and to meet after** all these years— two old women! When I was last in this room you **wore** a mauve silk and it went so well with your complexion—you used to have such a beautiful colour and there was not a line on your face—or at least there were only a few; but now—who would think you were the same creature ? "

"You are more fortunate than I am," said Mrs. Portcullis, smiling horribly, "for you have a grown-up daughter to remind us of your lost attractions ! "

Blanche gasped, but although she felt the weight of Charlotte's blow she was not sufficiently skilled herself to appreciate its science.

"Oh," she said, growing red, "do you mean Teresa ? "

"Surely," quoth her sister, in a tone of horror, "there is but one I could mean ! "

Lady Warcop lifted her eyes and gazed as bravely as she dared at the miniature of the late William Duncan Portcullis which reposed on Charlotte's adamantine breast. This miniature, however, only served to produce in Blanche the kind

of panic which we may suppose
would fill **any** weak creature who
saw scalps adorning the person of
a warlike adversary.

"Tell me about Teresa," said
Mrs. Portcullis, choosing the subject most humiliating to her sister.

"She is at school."

"I understood she was in a
convent."

"Yes," faltered Lady Warcop,
"there is a school in the convent!"

"From a Romish point of view
such equivocation, I know, is not
considered disgraceful. Our religion, thank God, is not so easy!
You must **send for** her at once.
She is, **if** I remember rightly, eighteen and a half, and, not to hurt
your feelings, she can only retrieve
the lamentable circumstances of
her birth by making a good marriage. Although we have not met,
my dear Blanche, you have been

ever in my mind, and the altera-
tion in my appearance which you
find so startling is, no doubt, mi-
raculously evident to you because
your disgrace **has** been its sole
cause. Blessed with the kindest
of husbands and a good conscience, I have had, nevertheless, a
constant sorrow—that sorrow was
my sister's shame. Oh! do not
suppose I utter this **as a** reproach!
I name it because I think my long
years of grief give me the right to
express a very strong opinion on
the subject of your unhappy child's
education and future. Your own
sense will tell you that she must
be guarded far more strictly than
other girls. For instance, she must
not be seen at balls, theaters, race-
courses, country houses, or the
like, but must rest content with
dinners, oratorios, and good works
for the poor."

"You are too kind," said Lady Warcop, who had listened with astonishing patience to her sister's speech, "but I do not wish Teresa to leave the convent at present. She is extremely happy there, and I can only wish that at her age I might have found such a peaceful home far removed from the temptations and wickedness of this deceitful world! As for her marrying, I have too much reason to regret my own early marriage—the cause of all my trouble—to wish the poor child to risk a similar mistake."

"You did not leave dear Douglas for a richer man!" said Mrs. Portcullis, in a tone which implied that if Blanche had made a more discreet choice, her sin would have been less odious.

"Perhaps not," said Blanche; "but I left a man who did not understand me for one who—— You know, Charlotte, that Sidney could make himself very agreeable. There were many women who would have been far readier than I was to run away with him. Indeed, he has often said that it was my resistance which chiefly excited his admiration, and if I had not been so firm on *my* side, he would not have been so determined on *his*. I saw that from the first, and I cannot tell you the *hours* we spent arguing the matter from every possible point of view. He used a great deal of persuasion (and you may be sure I would not have wasted a thought on him if he had not), but I took the final step with great reluctance. We may have been foolish, but we meant no wrong. I was unhappy; he was kind to **me**; we were both young."

"Sir Sidney was certainly young," said Mrs. Portcullis. "As for you, I can make no excuse on the ground

2

of your age, for I always blame the woman in such cases, and, to my mind, it does not matter in the least whether she be sixteen or sixty. But it is a subject I must refuse to discuss with you, since, in the nature of things, it is inexpressibly painful **to me.** Let us return to the pressing and all-important question of Teresa's future. I would suggest that you send for her at once, and then you may bring her with you to a small dinner I am giving on the twentieth. The Dundrys, the Paget-Herons, **and a** few other old friends of mine are coming."

Blanche, who had been hopelessly hoping these many years for a smile of recognition from the Lady Dundry (known among her intimates as "Arabella, dowdy, but exclusive"), no sooner heard that magic name than her whole demeanor changed. The little dignity and resolution she had assumed fell like a veil, and it **was** soon agreed between the two women that Teresa should be sent for on the morrow.

"The nuns must bring her **to** London," said Blanche, "for Sidney hates the Channel, and it is death to *me*."

Yet she had crossed it on the great occasion of her elopement.

III.

Four days after this interview between Lady Warcop and her sister, Sir Sidney might have been seen making his way towards Bedford Row. In person he was unusually handsome, his head and features reminding one **in** a striking degree of the popular representation of Cicero, while his extraordinarily brilliant blue eyes and lively hair did full justice to his Celtic origin. As in the case of Agamemnon, there

were many men taller than he, but
in a crowd he was not to be matched
for grace and majesty of movement.
There was, however, a certain
studied ease in his gestures, a pre-
meditated charm in his manner,
which to those who disagreed with
his politics made insincerity seem
the sincerest thing about him. But
if he had not a guileless soul, he had
at least immaculate linen, which so
dazzled the spectator by its purity
that to a cynical mind it might have
seemed that in this generation a
good laundress is more useful than
a clean record.

When Sir Sidney entered the pri-
vate office of Mr. Robert Waddilove
(of the firm of Waddilove, Shorncliffe, Shorncliffe, and Pride, Soli-
citors), Mr. Waddilove rose from
his chair, bowed, and remembered
the time when he would have called
on his client and trifled away a

pleasant morning with scandal, choice cigars, incomparable sherry, and a "little matter of business," which came last and was invariably left " to your discretion, Waddilove." But now, oh heavy change! Even as the Baronet entered he looked at his watch.

"Not detain you ten minutes," he said, speaking rapidly, and as though he were dictating a telegram. "Not legal, but domestic. **Wife** most annoying. Teresa coming home. Wife in hysterics every time girl's name is mentioned. No living in the house."

Waddilove rubbed his chin. He was a man of middle age, short, but so compactly built that to look at him made one think of bricks and cement. His quick brown eyes were remarkable for their curiously mingled expression of shrewdness, scepticism, and good humor, and

his wry mouth showed that if he
drank in life like a worldling, he
swallowed it like a philosopher.
His nose was of the penetrating
order, and seemed to have jutted
prematurely from his forehead,
which was broad and thoughtful.

His under-lip twitched a little at
the close of Sir Sidney's remarks.
"We will call this a friendly chat,"
he said quietly.

"Eh?" said the Baronet, with
a radiant air, "not professional?
Well, after all, it is not a legal matter. But you are quite sure? Still,
between such old friends any question of business and that sort of
thing is unpleasant. Conversation
becomes restrained at once." He
chose a chair, and sat in statuesque
ease.

"You know what women are,"
he said.

Waddilove closed his eyes as

though he would exclude a painful vision.

"You know what my wife is," continued Sir Sidney.

The lawyer looked grave, in the formal manner appropriate to the discussion of family skeletons—a manner not so much indicative of pity, which might verge too much on the familiar, as of concern—disinterested, brain-felt concern.

"I have nothing to say against Lady Warcop," said her husband. "She has many excellent qualities, but on the subject of Teresa she is a—what-do-you-call-'em?"

"An enigma," suggested Waddilove, but in a voice so modulated that had the word been unwelcome it might have passed for a cough.

"That is the thing," said Sir Sidney, "an enigma. And to turn against her own daughter, her only child! She has not seen her since

she was born; there has always
been some **excuse**. But now she
has suddenly sent for her, and God
knows why, for no sooner had she
written the letter than she declared
she would not have her in the
house. Damn it all! it is *my* house
and *my* daughter! When a man
cannot have his own way in his
own house, then—then it comes to
this—somebody must give in. If I
say, ' Blanche, I am going to put
my foot down,' she begins to cry.
She says, too, that her hair is turning grey with silent worry. And
you know, Waddilove, she is never
silent, and she is no longer so young
that a grey hair or two seems extraordinary. But there are quarrels
between us from morning till night,
and I cannot allow it. Life is not
worth living. Why did she send
for the girl if she did not want her?
Where's the consistency? As I told

Blanche this morning—'Blanche,' I said, as kindly as possible—I did not want a scene, as you may imagine—'Blanche,' I said, 'if you will tell me why you sent for Teresa, in the first place'——But, God bless your soul! before the words were out of my mouth she flew at me like a tigress. And what do you think she said? 'What! do you begrudge your own child her rightful home? I suppose you do not wish to be reminded of the past. For it was all your fault, although I have had all the blame.' Imagine her referring to dead and gone matters in that offensive manner! And **she** was the one who had been abusing the poor child—not I. I ask you what could any man do with a woman like that?"

"It is a very difficult question," said Waddilove.

"And there is nothing to be gained

by a separation," said Sir Sidney,
"because she is so unreasonable,
and can neither make head nor tail
of the law. There is no peace for
me this side of the grave."

"What does Lady Warcop suggest?" said Waddilove. "What are
her wishes in the matter?"

"God knows!" said Sir Sidney.
"If I knew what she wanted we
might come to some understanding.
But one moment she says one thing
and the next another. My health
will not bear it much longer. What
do you advise me to do in the meantime?"

"You must be firm," said Waddilove.

"Impossible ; quite impossible.
Whenever I speak firmly she begins
to cry. You see, she is a gentle,
sweet-tempered sort of woman by
nature. One does not like to be
brutal."

" Have you tried persuasion ? "

"I have tried everything—coax-ing, threatening, commanding, and exhorting ; jokes, presents, theatres, and sermons ; reading, singing, playing, and, so far **as** that goes, praying. No husband could do more to make his wife happy—un-less, indeed, he blew his brains out ! "

" I am afraid," said Waddilove, "you must make up your mind to endure these annoyances."

Sir Sidney sighed heavily and rose from his chair. " Before **I** married her," he said, " she was as mild as an angel. She was a little contrary now and again, but one kind word, and she would do anything. Douglas Cockburn never understood that, and tried bullying. Now I see, however, that there were faults on both sides. Of course, I would not say as much to any one

else. This is a judgment on me,
Waddilove, and if I did not know it
was a judgment I could not bear it
another day. As it is, I will face it
out to the bitter end. Good-bye."

He left the office with the uneasy
idea that he had been talking too
freely, and, as a consequence, he
began to hate Waddilove as a pry-
ing, impertinent fellow—a fellow to
be avoided. What right had he to
ask so many questions? But it had
been a relief to speak out : to utter
his feelings ; to rid himself even by
a straw's weight of that load of
sorrow, disappointment, dissatisfac-
tion, and weariness, the bearing of
which, after all, proved that his poor
fragment of a soul had still its use
in the scheme of salvation.

IV.

LADY WARCOP, meanwhile, was
pacing the floor of her boudoir. In

her hand she held the photograph of a singularly plain little girl, who stood in a cork grotto staring at a stuffed dog. This portrait of Teresa had been taken some ten years before, and Blanche had lacked the courage to send for another. And now, without warning, to be obliged to present *this* to the world! It was too hard, too bitter, too outrageous. Was ever woman called upon to suffer such mortification? As for motherly feelings, what were they? How could she love a creature she had never seen? Some one had once shown her an infant, but she had felt too ill to notice the piteous object. She did not even understand that it was her own. There was so much cant and nonsense talked about maternal instinct. A cab drove up to the door; with a cry, her Ladyship rushed to the window. Thank goodness, it

was only Sidney. What suffering !
What suspense ! One more day like
this, and she would be on her
death-bed.

"Ah ! so you have come at last,
Sidney ? " Where had he been all
the morning ? She made few demands on his time, but she certainly
thought that in common decency
and merely for the sake of ap-
pearances he would have remained
with her to receive poor darling
Teresa. It was true that she had
not yet arrived, but this did not
alter the fact that he *might* have
missed her. Poor child ! a stranger
in her own father's house ! But the
world was a cruel place, and she,
for her part, was sick and tired
of it. If it were not for Teresa,
who needed a mother's care, she
was by no means sure that she
might not seek a speedy way out of
it. Suicide, of course, was wicked,

but God was never hard on women. He understood them : men did not. . . . Was that the bell ?

"Go and meet her," said Blanche. "Try and look affectionate. I want the poor little thing to think we are glad to see her. As for me, I feel too ill and extraordinary to move."

As she spoke, however, the door was opened, and two nuns, followed by a young girl, were ushered in. Her Ladyship flushed and paled, and, without speaking, with tears raining down her cheeks, took the girl in her arms, tenderly, closely, as only a mother can.

Sir Sidney rubbed his eyes, almost fearing to rest them on a scene so beautiful, so new in his experience. Blanche seemed to him transfigured, and he saw in that brief moment the woman she might have been : all the fair ambitions she had forgotten, all the good impulses she had not obeyed flashed their pure light on her countenance.

Like some guilty creature, he left the room.   He was the only sinner there.

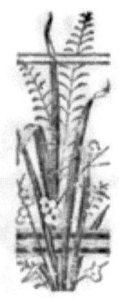

CHARACTERS OF THE BOOK.

LORD TWACORBIE.

SIDNEY WICHE, M.P., *Proprietor and Editor of " The Watchman."*

NICHOLAS T. VAN HUYSTER, *an American millionaire and poet.*

CAPTAIN SAVILLE ROOKES.

SIR VENTRY COXE, *a widower.*

LADY TWACORBIE, *his sister.*

THE HON. FELICIA GORM, *her step-daughter.*

TERESA WARCOP, *an heiress, cousin to Lady Twacorbie.*

LADY MALLINGER, *a very young widow.*

LUFFY, *the head-gardener.*

SPALDING, *the butler.*

MRS. DANBY *the housekeeper.*

THE scene is laid at Arden Lodge, the country seat of Lord Twacorbie, in Mertfordshire. The action takes place in the course of twenty-four hours.

" *One day is with the Lord as a thousand years, and a thousand years as one day.*"

3

A BUNDLE OF LIFE.

I.

HE dining-room in Arden Lodge was superbly furnished with a silver chandelier. This splendid object was of such incomparable interest that Lord Twacorbie, who was a man of taste no less than an economist, had the walls which formed its background, bare, the floor beneath covered with a plain drugget, and the tables and chairs in the apartment of the simplest design. On the same artistic principle, he gave large dinners, at which the rarest, indeed, un-heard-of delicacies, (which were as disagreeable to the palate as they were interesting to the explorer and antiquarian), formed the brief but sufficient menu.

On a certain evening in the early spring of 189–, one of these dinners had taken place with unusual suc-cess, possibly because most of the thirty guests were persons of im-portance, probably because some roast mutton had, by a new cook's judicious mistake, formed a vulgar but stimulating addition to the choice viands of the banquet. The ladies had left the table, and the fifteen men who remained sighed, some with relief, some with regret, some from the force of example, and some because they could dine no more that day.

Lord Twacorbie was a gentleman whom food did not nourish, and

whose airy shapelessness made him
seem in some way symbolic of the
universe when it was without form,
and void. To-night he fluttered a
smile like the sun's on a March
morning, and **surveyed** the company with the feverish gaiety of one
who is too seriously bored to risk
showing languor. He was of all
men the last to entertain a table,
yet few attempted the task so often,
and no one could have been more
ignorant of his failures. He started
a conversation **on** the Early Mar-
riages Bill, and quoted, with in-
spired inaccuracy, a speech recently
made on that subject by his friend,
Sidney **Wiche.** Wiche, who happened to be present, endured his
host's recital with the air of one ac-
customed to suffering ; at its close
his countenance had something
humorous, pathetic, and sublime—
St. Lawrence on the gridiron saying,

"Turn me! This side is done!" must have looked just so. The editor of *The Watchman* was a man of slender frame and with fewer inches than the ordinary; a small mortal whose boundless spirit—imprisoned yet not impatient for release—gazed through his eyes. His pale face, dull brown hair and duller beard, and the absence in his manner of all that marks the creature of many fashions and one epoch, had made him more famous for his insignificance than any of his contemporaries for their distinction. He was about seven-and-thirty, and hard work had made him look much older.

Two men who sat at the far end of the table seized the advantage of their position, and, talking in undertones, studied him with lively interest.

"Of course, he is clever," said

the elder of the two ; "or, at least, he is a great man for the mob. There is a distinction between greatness and being great in the eyes of *a certain class*." The speaker, Sir Ventry **Coxe, had the** so-called aristocratic air sometimes found in men of middle-class extraction, but unknown amongst the old nobility. Very young girls, sentimental women, and men **of** his own stamp, thought him extremely handsome : his features were bold and well-defined, his dark eyes could express any drawing-room emotion with really excellent effect ; his thin, straight lips suggested his refined tastes to those who understand culture as leanness and vulgarity as curves.

" What do they think of Wiche in America ? " continued the Baronet.

" They wonder that he does not marry," replied his companion ;

"there are so many pretty women in England."

Mr. Nicholas T. Van Huyster was a young man about eight-and-twenty, tall, slight, dark, and clean-shaven. His face was not at first sight sympathetic, but, on the other hand, he did not have the aggressive air of one who is conscious that he must be known to be appreciated.

"Wiche is not popular in society," said Sir Ventry. "He has no presence, no manners, no small talk."

"No," answered the American, "he is not that modern of each May so beloved of dining London."

"His family is nothing," said Sir Ventry. "His mother was a person of no education, who lived with an art-critic called Wiche. By the by, can you imagine a more miserable occupation than this scribbling about art? What is Art? Madness in most cases, and mere frippery in others. And only one man here and there makes it pay. Look at Nature, I say, if you want beautiful pictures. But I was telling you about this fellow. It seems he was christened Sidney Wiche; his mother said that his name was at least Christian if it was not legal ! I am thankful to say I never met her. I do not pretend to be a saint, but a woman without a conscience strikes me dumb ! I feel that there is nothing more to say ! "

"Conscience is the name which the orthodox give to their prejudices," said Van Huyster. "But have you ever heard," he went on, drawing out his pocket-book, "that Wiche's father left a very eccentric will? I received this from New York last night." He handed a newspaper cutting to Sir Ventry, who read the following :—

"*Sidney Wiche was to be first a Christian, then a scholar, and in course of time a philosophical politician. He was not to marry, 'but,' ran the strange document, 'should he feel drawn towards the married state let him give the matter his best consideration for a no less term than five years, since marriage is of all subjects the one most darkened by fallacy, falsehood, and false sentiment.' During this period of prayer and reflection he was to read 'neither poets nor romancers, but St. Thomas Aquinas, Cardinal Newman, and the great historians, who, between them, would so satisfy his soul, his manliness, and his common-sense that after their company any feminine prattler would seem a plague rather than a treasure.' He was to shun 'as he would the devil, learned ladies, ladies with artistic gifts, ladies who talked religion, and ladies who were not* *ladies !' **In conclusion, he** was earnestly exhorted to practice the pious exercise of meditating for two hours daily on his own nothingness !"*

"Very interesting," remarked Sir Ventry ; "but interesting things **are** never true."

"And the truth is only convincing when it is told by an experienced liar," observed Nicholas.

"Old Wiche **has** been dead for some time," said Sir Ventry, "and I never heard that he left Sidney either means of support or instructions ; it ought to be made known if he did. One likes to hear that a man has behaved like a gentleman in such matters. Unfortunately, he died abroad, and his affairs were **managed by** these Italian scoundrels. One can get nothing out **of** them. I must say I like English straightforwardness."

"*The Watchman* must bring in a large income," said Van Huyster.

"Undoubtedly," replied Sir Ventry. "But what a rag the paper is! These Radicals are ruining the nation."

"I thought Wiche was a member of your own party."

"My own party," said Sir Ventry, "is not necessarily my own politics! As a man," he went on, after a pause, "I like the fellow well enough, and now that he has pushed his way into the world we all try to forget his origin. But with every desire to be fair, I cannot bring myself to regard him as a suitable match for any relative of my own. It is only too well-known that he admires my sister's step-daughter, Miss Gorm."

"That does not surprise me," said Van Huyster, fetching a deep sigh, "she is lovely. Her face is so bright **yet** so delicate—a star wrapped in gauze ! "

Sir Ventry dropped his lower jaw, but recovered it on remembering that the millionaire wrote poetry, very bad poetry, **too.** " Felicia is certainly good-looking," he said ; "perhaps you are aware that her mother, the former Lady Twacorbie, was an American. She made Twacorbie an excellent wife, however, greatly improved the estate and was very much liked **by** the Royalties. She died young."

" Good wives so often do," murmured Van Huyster, " perhaps that **is** one of their brightest virtues."

Sir Ventry abhorred anything in the nature of satire—it seemed to him a convenient name for offensive and unmistakable allusions to **his** own character and career. On this occasion he wondered whether Van Huyster was aware that he, **too,**

Sir Ventry Coxe, had in his day buried some sixty-three inches of weary perfection.   He decided to ignore the remark.

"One can see," he said, "that Felicia is extremely un-English : her manners are a little crude.   But I like a woman who can talk : a man wants to be amused, he does not want to wear his brains out amusing a wife !"

At this point Lord Twacorbie rose up from the table.

The pantry was immediately behind the dining-room—and here, at the close of the dinner, Spalding, the butler, the head-gardener, Luffy, and Mrs. Danby, the housekeeper, were engaged in conversation of an even more instructive nature than that indulged in by Lord Twacorbie and his distinguished company.

"Who came down from town this evening?" asked Luffy.

"Sir Ventry, Mr. Wiche, Captain Rookes, and this new American, Mr. Van Huyster," said the housekeeper.

"And who are the women?" continued Luffy.

"Miss Warcop for one," said Mrs. Danby. "Between ourselves her ladyship is on the matchmaking hop again. But there—when did she ever pull anything off what you may call satisfactory? She's too hopeful. And say what you like, Luffy, it doesn't do to be hopeful in this world. Expect nothing, I say!" The widow shook her head, and heaved her breast, and hurled a poignant glance at Spalding, who had been shuddering on the brink of matrimony for twelve and a half years.

"It might be a very good thing for Sir Ventry if Miss Warcop would have him," said Spalding; "but the question arises in my mind, will she? If she would take my advice she would stay single!"

"Everybody is not so wrapt up in theirselves as you are," said Mrs. Danby, tartly.

"If I was a woman," murmured Spalding, in a weak voice, "the man doesn't live that I would sacrifice my peace of mind for. Men are not worth so much thought. The devotion of women is something awful to think of."

"It is," sighed Luffy, whose wife had a jealous temperament, "it is."

"I can say this much," said Mrs. Danby: "when Miss Warcop marries she will not choose a conceited, self-seeking, cold-hearted, unfeeling *half-a-man* like Sir Ventry! I would not look at him—no, not if he draped me in diamonds from head to foot! Mr. Wiche is the man for her."

"Not he," said Spalding, "he's got his eye on Lady Mallinger."

"If he was to roll his eyes at Lady Mallinger from now till Dooms-day," said Mrs. Danby, "I should still say that he and Miss Warcop were made for each other. And, what is more, they will marry. Whoever lives longest will see the most. I know what I know. If God Almighty intends a couple to marry that marriage will come off. The man can't help himself. Just you bear that in mind!"

She left them, and neither of the men had the courage to smile. They talked instead of the new Cemetery, and grew cheerful on the subject of coffins.

II.

ARDEN LODGE in Mertford-shire is a large, white building surrounded by beautiful grounds, and facing the finest scenery in the county. This is saying a great deal, for although Mertford is flat and not at all wild or what is called romantic, its rivers and fields, gardens and woods, toy-like farms and shady parks are, for their kind, the prettiest in the world. And one can only find such peculiar prettiness in England; it is so well-disposed, calm and unsuggestive— inspiring neither passionate senti-

ments, nor unearthly music, nor
flaming words, but what, in some
opinions, may be better than all
these—a dreamless, ineffable drowsi-
ness.

On the morning after the dinner-
party, a lady and gentleman were
strolling on the Terrace which led
by wide steps on to the lawn of
Lord Twacorbie's residence. The
lady was Miss Warcop : her escort
was Sidney Wiche.

Teresa was no longer in her first
youth, and she had never been
pretty : her oval face was colorless,
heavy black eyebrows overhung her
hazel eyes ; mouth, nose, and chin
were too obviously mouth, nose,
and chin. She was remarkable,
however, and only needed a repu-
tation for wickedness to make her
considered curiously fascinating.

As these two came down the steps,
they were commenting on the

weather, the unusual warmth, seeing
it was but Easter, and the freshness
of the air.   When they reached the
lawn, they walked in silence to a
seat, sat down and stared at the
landscape.   They were evidently
old friends.

"Well," said Wiche, at last, "is
the most practical woman in the
world, dreaming?"

"I was thinking of you," she answered, looking at him with such
frank, unclouded affection that he
blushed to think how little he de-
served it.   He might have made
some answer, but as she spoke they
both heard the rustle of silk skirts :
the sound grew nearer : at last a
lady, charmingly attired in a gown
which suggested gray vapor and
sunlight, approached them.   She
presented a strange effect of bril-
liance, fragility, and mistiness : her
features were soft, and her head in

profile seemed rather a shadow in
the air than something real or human.   But the shadow was plainly
womanish—one could never have
mistaken it for an angel's.   Her
skin was fair, her hair light brown,
her eyes blue, sapphirine, deep, a
little troubled : she gazed at Wiche,
he gazed at her ; Teresa watched the
meeting with some uneasiness.

"I did not know that the glare
was so great," she said, faintly ;
"I should have brought my par-
asol."

" Let me fetch it ! " said Wiche.

She thanked him as, with an admirable semblance of good humor,
he left them.

"You met Mr. Wiche some years
ago, did you not ? " Teresa asked,
turning to Lady Mallinger : "did
you know him at all well ? "

"That would depend on what
you call *well*," said the younger

woman. Her voice was strangely melodious : to hear it was to think of the fabulous singing of fabulous sirens. If she babbled of brick-dust, one thought only of lute-strings. For this reason she was never quoted accurately.

"I mean," said Teresa, " were you great friends ? "

"I should not **say that.**"

"I thought I saw him looking at you rather often during dinner **last** evening."

"Did he ? " said Lady Mallinger. " I hope my hair was dressed prop-erly. My maid **is** in love just at present, and she makes me quite frightful. It is **not** that she is ma-licious, but Love is so distracting." Smiling sweetly, she looked first at the trees, then at the grass, **and** finally at Teresa. "In some **ways,**" she went **on,** "I am rather sorry **to** renew Mr. Wiche's acquaintance :

we have nothing in common—
absolutely nothing. He has **the**
instincts of a Turk : he does not
believe in a woman's intellect.
Sometimes I wish I really **was**
stupid and lived in a harem ! "

" My dear ! " said Teresa.

" I do, indeed : women were not
made to struggle and strive. They
ought only to be fed and clothed
and petted. But I thought other-
wise **once**. **Before** my marriage I
was anxious to work out a career :
I wanted to be artistic : I thought I
might become a famous actress.
Ah, to think of those days when I
was hoping and dreaming, when
my thoughts were my achievements,
when the future seemed so far and
the present so eternal ! " Her voice
trembled, she flushed and then grew
pale : one could imagine that she
was struggling in a very hurricane
of lost possibilities. " But when

work began in earnest," she continued, "when art became a task, and dreaming, waste of time, I confess I grew sick of ambition. I only wanted to sit idle in the market-place. And so I married, and danced, and dressed, and chattered : I gave up thinking—it made me too miserable." Teresa had an extraordinary power of winning confidences : perhaps because she rarely talked.

"A woman's mission is to play the fool," continued Lady Mallinger, "and that is why she can only lead a man so long as she does not love him. On the instant she loves, she must be honest or die : she loses all discretion : she quarrels when she should cajole, smiles when she should frown, utters ugly truth when she should tell pretty lies : she cannot flatter, she cannot pretend—in fact, she can do nothing but love—and that beyond sense." Commanding was not the word for Lady Mallinger's manner: yet there was that in her air which insisted, which brooked no denial, which said plainly enough: "What I think must be, because I was not born to be disappointed!"

"I do not agree with you," said Teresa, "because if I loved a man I would have no desire to lead him. I could only pray that I might not prove his stumbling-block, and that we might help each other to do right rightly. Life is so hard to live alone."

"Oh, if I only dared to be natural," exclaimed Lady Mallinger; "if I only dared to tell all I think, and feel, and know. If I could only drop this tedious gossiping and grinning! I am not tired of living, but I am tired of my body—of this mummy-case. When I was a child,

I felt old ; now I am a woman, I feel young. I want to go back to the youth of the world : I want the time when love was the only happiness, and folly the highest wisdom ! "

" Did you ever talk like this to Mr. Wiche ? " said Teresa.

" Of course not," said Lady Mallinger. " I only talk nonsense to men ! "

" Dear me ! Yet I daresay they like it. But I promised to show Mr. Wiche the primrose path. As you do not care for him, I will meet him half-way. See ! he is coming now." She rose from her seat and hastened across the lawn in the direction of the house. Lady Mallinger sat smiling to herself : she had never suffered from jealousy, and she thought it the drollest of passions. She was on the verge of laughter when Captain Rookes appeared on the Terrace. He was undeniably handsome : his features had that harmonious irregularity which is so much more like truth than beauty, so much more life-like, sinner-like, and love-like than perfection. His eyes flashed fire and sentiment—youth lacking either is dull—melancholy had added a force to their magic.

"Are you sure," he said anxiously, as he approached Lady Mallinger, "are you sure that it is discreet to meet here where every one can see us?"

"Of course," said her ladyship, whose whole bearing and manner changed, and who now assumed an infantile, prattling, and pouting simplicity; "of course, I hate out-of-the-way corners."

"Speak a little lower, darling," said Saville, "there may be some gardeners about."

"That would not matter."

"Not matter? My dear Lilian, you do not know the world. If the world knew how much we loved each other, it would grow suspicious."

"Why? Numbers of people love each other."

"Yes," said the Captain, "but we are not like other people. I love you too well to ask you to marry me and so drag you down to a miserable shabby-genteel existence."

"I do not mind being poor, Saville," said Lady Mallinger, eagerly. "Before my marriage, Papa only allowed me sixty pounds a year for my clothes, and every one said how well I managed. That, I know, was as a girl, and, of course, a married woman has to dress more—in a sense—but a handsome mantle goes a long way. Lady Twacorbie has worn that

satin and lace thing at least four
seasons : she has had the sleeves
altered, and it has been re-lined
with a different color, but it is the
same cloak ! And I am tired of
marrying for money : it is not **as**
though I had not tried it.   No one
can say that I gave the least trouble
when they married me to Charles—
although I never did admire red
hair, and he was the worst dancer
in his regiment. I know he was
most civil to poor Papa, but after
all he was not so rich as they
thought him, and it would have
been wiser, perhaps, if I had remained single a little longer.   But
you, Saville, I could be poor with
you : you are so sympathetic, and
you wrote me such a beautiful letter
when Charles died.   I am sure, too,
that he would **have** been pleased
with that lovely wreath !   And—
and I cannot forget the old days

when we made toffee together in
the schoolroom at home.   Do you
remember ? "

Saville tried to look as though the
toffee episode had for him thoughts
too deep for utterance.   He flung
cautious glances about the scene
and then hastily pressed her hand.

"How can you ask?" he said :
"But believe me, dearest Lilian,
our only duty is renunciation.   I
mean, we must forget our love, and
if we can, each other.   I have been
waiting months to find words for all
this : it seemed unutterable.   Truth
is difficult, and the less one speaks
it the harder it grows.   I have lied
when I pretended to be happy.   I
find it easier after all to admit that
I am in despair.   Yet not despair—
because I feel that honor is still
dearer to me than your society.
The thought is hackneyed, but so
are the commandments.   Some day

you will meet some excellent, well-meaning man who will have a fortune worth offering you. Perhaps he will not be much to look at and he may not be polished in his manners. I daresay, **too,** that he **will** often say and **do** much which will jar on your refined taste. But polish is not everything!"

"I cannot live," cried Lady Mallinger, "in an unpolished atmosphere!"

"You see, my darling, we all have to endure disagreeable things in this life; money and love never seem to go together."

"We should have fifteen hundred **a** year," whimpered Lilian.

"What is that, my dear child?" **said** Saville. "Two thousand **is** the lowest income I can conceive myself marrying on. As I **have** said, if I cared **for you in the** ordinary, **vulgar way,** I might risk

everything and urge you to ruin my
whole life—and perhaps your own
as well. So, darling, is it fair to
tempt me?"

"I do not want to tempt you,"
said Lady Mallinger. "I only want
to talk sensibly. Please, please,
dear Saville, do not say that I am
tempting you. I would not be so
wicked, for I am sure you only
want to do right, and men know
much more about honor and in-
comes and things like that than
women do !"

Sweet, submissive, believing, un-
assertive Lilian, of a type all but
extinct ! Where would he find such
another? He rose from his seat in
agitation, feeling, for the moment,
that he might in an emergency
show the splendid indiscretion of a
hero. But the mood passed, and
with it a great deal of Lady Mallinger's folly. Something else, in-

definable, chilling, deadly, took its place in her soul. She, too, stood up, and in silence they surveyed a far-distant and sleeping cow.

"You see, Lilian," Saville stammered at last.

"I see it all clearly," she replied. "I only wonder why I did not see it before. It would be the greatest mistake in the world for us to marry!"

This remark cut him to the heart: he flushed, his whole aspect suffered.

"No woman," he said, "could say such a thing to a man she loved. You cannot care for me."

"I do indeed care for you, Saville," she said, "please believe me."

Rookes, happily, did not need much persuasion to convince him. "This world is a beastly place," he burst forth. "It has everything to

5

make one happy except happiness. Look at us! We are young, we love each other, we have the same tastes, and we are in the same set. How we could enjoy life! But we cannot afford it."

"It is hard," said Lilian, "terribly hard. I daresay, though, that is all for the best."

"I must go away," said Saville: "I see too much of you; it is too tantalizing! But hush! here comes Felicia."

"How well you know her step!" exclaimed Lilian.

III.

FELICIA GORM was a young girl about seventeen, with large blue eyes, small regular features, and rosy cheeks ; to-day she was even rosier than usual.

"Mamma would be so grateful if you would talk to Mr. Van Huyster," she said to Saville ; "he is asking so many questions about England, and no one can answer him."

When Rookes had left them, Felicia tried to look disinterested. "Have you ever noticed," she said, "how easily he blushes. . . . It does not mean anything—although Mama says that men only blush nowadays to be mistaken for Christians! I am sure that is not the case with Captain Rookes. . . . Do you like him?"

"We are half-cousins!"

The young girl sat down by her side. "Dear Lady Mallinger," she said, "I am dreadfully unhappy. But I am so fond of you; I am sure you will help me."

"Indeed, I will. What is troubling you?"

"Where shall I begin? Mama sent for me this morning. I felt it was to be a serious conversation because she wore her coronet brooch. She told me that if Mr. Wiche asked me to marry him, I was to say yes. Think of it! It seems they have arranged it all between them; they think he is growing too democratic, and now he has refused a Baronetcy he has become more popular than ever. They say it would be such an excellent thing if he married a Peer's daughter, and Mama says I must sacrifice myself for the sake of the country. I am sure that marriage into *our* family will not change his opinion of the House of Lords ! I have no influence with him, but Mama says I must **try to** have one ; that he must be very fond of me or he would not stay here. Every one knows that he detests visiting as a rule. I believe he is in love with *you*, but Mama says that is an absurd idea, because he knew you before you married Lord Mallinger, and he **is** not the kind of man who would fancy your style of beauty in a wife. He is always staring at you at any rate. Then I said he seemed great friends with Teresa ; but then, as Mama says, dear Teresa is almost ugly, and if he had intended to marry her for her money, he would have done so long ago! So I suppose I must be the one after all, and in the end I shall have to accept him. But— but I shall always love Saville best!"

"Saville?" exclaimed Lady Mallinger, in astonishment. "Saville?"

"If you knew him as I do, you would not wonder that I love him," said Felicia, blushing deeply, "he is so chivalrous, so noble, so un- selfish, just like King Arthur in Lord Tennyson. And to hear him speak of women! He thinks we are all angels. I am so afraid, dear Lady Mallinger, lest he may be disappointed in us, because we are not all angels, are we?"

Lady Mallinger all this time had kept her eyes on the ground, and,

but for **her** gentle breathing, betrayed no signs of animation. At
the girl's question, however, she
stirred.

"Has Saville **told** you—has he
said—has he **spoken**——?"

"**He** knows that I love him,"
said Felicia, faintly.

"But has he asked you to be his
wife?"

"Not **in** so many words, **but**
words are not everything. **He is**
not rich; he is afraid **people might**
say—you know what they always
say. Once he told me he wished I
had no money—that I was **poor**
and unknown. Oh, I understand
him so **well.**"

"I am **sure** your family would
not care **for the match,"** said **Lilian,**
at last; "and evidently they have
set their hearts on Wiche. Wiche
is rather odd, but I was only thinking last night what **a** fine face he

has : he would make you a kind
husband, and you would be
quite contented—after a little."
The foolishest of mortals may often
be startled into a certain sagacity ;
and Felicia's innocence had the
effect of rousing Lady Mallinger's
common-sense which, though un-
disciplined and kitten-like, was still
promising.

"No doubt," she continued, looking gravely at the girl's anxious
face, "Saville is most agreeable,
and it is very pleasing to think that
such a handsome, popular fellow is
in love with one. But would you
feel so flattered if he were plain : if
you heard, for instance, that he
was fickle, mercenary, and treach-
erous ! "

"But I might hear that of Wiche,
too," said Felicia. "You see, dear
Lady Mallinger, I must believe in
some man or I could not marry at

all ! And I would rather be deceived by Saville than adored by Sidney Wiche ! "

" That is absurd. I should be very wrong to encourage you in such ideas. When you are older you will see how foolish it is to indulge in these fancies ! "

" I am afraid you do not like Saville," said Felicia, suddenly.

" My dear little girl," said Lilian, with great dignity, " it is only because I am Saville's friend that I understand your point of view ! "

" Then why are you so angry with me for loving him ? I am sure you would not care for any one who was not noble and generous—you would not be his friend if he did not have fine qualities ! "

Conversation between a disillusioned devotee and an enthusiastic novice is always difficult : the disillusioned fears to be candid, and the enthusiast fears nothing ; one has not learnt enough, the other has **all to** learn.   This, then, was the situation of Lady Mallinger and Felicia. To one, Saville seemed a traitor; to the other, he was a being with neither body, soul, nor passions—a portable ideal who, at his sublimest, murmured, "I love you !"   Rookes was, **as a matter of** fact, a mortal whose good intentions and generous admiration **for** the admirable were not steady enough to carry the load of **a** fashionable education, **nor** robust enough to endure the nipping cruelty of society small talk. He feared his better instincts as the pious do their besetting sins, and when he was surprised into one of his natural virtues, his first precaution was to make it appear a polite vice.

"I will not **say one** word against Saville," said Lady Mallinger, **at** last. "I would rather not discuss him. In any case I can only implore you to obey your relatives : after all they must know best."

"Then," said Felicia, "it would be useless to ask you to help me."

"What can I do?" asked Lady Mallinger; "what is there that I could do ?"

"Well," said Felicia, " you see I am not yet engaged to Mr. Wiche. If he could only be made *not* to propose, everything would come right. Dear Lady Mallinger, if you would only distract his attention : you are so much prettier than I am, and I am sure he would be far more influenced by you than he ever could be by **me.** Oh, please promise me that you will try."

This suggestion was not without its charm. Lilian had a certain liking for Wiche : he appealed to her head rather than to her imagination, to her sympathies rather than to her senses : and, though he did not inspire her with poetic thoughts, he made the prose of her existence seem less like prose.

"Perhaps there would be no harm," she said, "and yet——"

"Oh, do promise," said Felicia, "my life and soul are bound up in it."

"One can tie a great many knots in one's life and soul," said Lady Mallinger.

"But love is so mysterious—so wonderful. It is the music of the world."

"It is a pity that it goes so often out of tune !" said Lilian. "Oh," she added suddenly, " our life is on so small a scale : everything seems so pretty ! Are women only born to fall in love with men like Saville Rookes? Why do we do these things ?"

"Because there is nothing else for us to do, I suppose," said Felicia.

"But think of all these clever women who paint pictures, and make speeches, and write for the papers, and sing, and act, and play. Ah, how grand it must be to have something serious to think of!"

"I believe they get very tired of it," said Felicia. "I am sure they are not half so happy as we are."

"Are we happy?" said Lilian.

"Of course we are," replied the young girl. "What a strange question!"

"Perhaps it is strange. I feel tired."

"And you look pale," said Felicia. "Let me fetch you my scent-bottle." She ran lightly across the lawn and up the Terrace steps without perceiving Saville who was returning from another direction.

He came close to Lady Mallinger and looked into her face.

"You do not look well," he said.

"I am well enough."

"Did that poor little thing bore you?"

"Not at all."

"Why are you so curt?"

"Am I?"

"Have I offended you?"

"Oh, no," said Lady Mallinger. "But you know quite well what Felicia has been talking about. You have acted abominably."

"What have I done?" asked **Rookes.** "Is it a crime to pay a few silly compliments to a child? She is hardly **more.** You are surely not jealous? You know **you** are the only woman I really care for. A man may love various women for various reasons at all times of his life, but he can only love once, one way. Each experience is to-

tally different, and absolutely new ;
only one, however, can be quite
satisfactory. Now to love you is
my second nature ; it is part of my
constitution. **If** you **do** not trust
me, **why** did you encourage me ? "

"Why ? " said Lady Mallinger,
with flashing eyes. "Why ? Do
you ask me why? I will not lie **to**
you. I loved you because I thought
you loved me—because I felt that
you would help me, *you*, who were
so much stronger, so much nobler,
so much braver than **I**. When you
said . . . when you seemed to think
I had some beauty, I longed to be
the most beautiful of all women,
that you might **be** proud **of** me : I
longed to be royal that **I** might
throw aside my royalty and **show**
the world that I would rather **be**
ruled by you than rule a kingdom :
I wanted a palace that I might leave
it and follow **you** into darkness and

poverty : I wished that we lived in times of danger that I might **save** you from death, that **I** might lie for you, hate for you, steal for you, die for you !　How I have loved you ! how have you deceived me ! I have nothing left but contempt **for** both of us. . . . Stay there !"

She walked a**way** alone, and as he felt too ashamed to follow her footsteps, he chose another path, and was therefore late for luncheon. A fact which showed the injured woman that her words had played some havoc with his conscience.

IV.

SIR VENTRY had been trying since noon to exchange a few words of immense importance with his sister. At last, in the drawing-room after luncheon, he found the moment. Teresa was playing the piano : Van Huyster and Felicia were within sight on the lawn. Lady Mallinger was cooing to some love-birds in a gilt cage which hung near the window. Lady Twacorbie sat at a little distance from the others, embroidering an altar-cloth. She was a being about five-and-thirty, dressed with

elegance, but with no attempt at
individuality. No doubt eleven out
of every dozen women in her own
station were wearing gowns of the
same hue, make, and texture. Her
hair was flaxen and arranged in the
artificial, half-grotesque style com-
manded by Court hair-dressers : at
a first glance she looked like a wax
doll—the unchanging expression,
the neat, set features, the unseeing
eyes, had not the divine impress.
Yet she lived and was a woman :
without her false curls, her whale-
bones, and her stare, she was even
beautiful : in unguarded moments,
she was witty. She was not
accomplished, however, and had no
force of will : the winds of opinion
blew her feather-like round the four
corners of her boudoir. But in her
way she was perfectly happy : she
sighed for no new experiences and
wept over no old ones : life pre-

6

sented no enigmas, and, feeling neither sorrow nor wonder, she had no need of philosophy. She read nothing, but was extraordinarily observant, and had **a most** tenacious memory **for** little things. For instance, **she** could quote whole conversations, and describe to a half-turn just how this one entered a room, that one shook hands, and the other sat down : she delighted afternoon callers by remembering how each liked **his or** her tea—A. never took sugar, **B.** liked three large lumps or four small ones, C. only drank hot water, D. could not bear the sight of cream, and so **on.** This **was** the lighter side of her character : she had **a** certain amount of sentiment, and would have made a devoted wife and mother of the primitive type. But the creatures of her world were bored by devotion, so she flirted in the most religious manner possible, and had an Infants' Bible-Class.

"My dear Charlotte," said Sir Ventry, "has it never occurred to you that Van Huyster is deeply interested in Felicia? I have observed it for days."

"You are always making unnecessary discoveries," replied his sister. "You know my plans with regard to Felicia. Wiche will certainly speak to her either to-day or to-morrow."

"Van Huyster is a far more desirable match; he is not only richer, but more tractable," said Sir Ventry. "If he were to speak first——"

"As you say," murmured her ladyship, "he is enormously rich."

"Precisely: that is my point. And he goes everywhere."

"But then Wiche is such a power in politics," said Lady Twacorbie;

" think what good we could do by our influence over him ! "

" The country would be far more grateful," said Sir Ventry, " if we helped Van Huyster to spend his money in a gentlemanly manner. However, it is your affair not mine. I have made a suggestion : act on it or not, as you please," and he strutted magnificently from her presence.

For some moments Lady Twacorbie did not ply her needle, but unpicked the stitches she had taken during the preceding conversation. At last she called Lilian. " Come and talk to me, my dear," she said ; " I have not had a word with you since breakfast. You see I drove Harold to the station "—(Lord Twacorbie had gone to town for a few days)—" He was so sorry to leave us." She glanced at Van Huyster and Felicia who passed the window. " We are so anxious about Felicia," she said ; " young girls are so flighty—is it reasonable to suppose that they are competent to select the right sort of man ? Ah, if women would only choose their husbands as carefully as they do their bonnets, how much brighter life would be ! "

" But, my dear Lady Twacorbie, what would you call the right sort of husband ? "

" A man," she replied, " with means, position, a good digestion, and sound principles : such a person, for instance, as this excellent, kind-hearted, and deserving Van Huyster ! "

" Van Huyster ! " said Lady Mallinger, in surprise.

" Yes. Have you observed how extremely attentive he is to Felicia ? "

" Perhaps I have, now you speak

of it," said Lilian, " but **I** thought Mr. Wiche——"

"Ah!" said Lady Twacorbie, " Mr. Wiche is all very well in his proper place. I have the greatest respect **for** his undeniable merits. I hope, however—I earnestly hope that he will not do anything rash. In fact, I may as well confess that I am in a difficulty. As Harold was obliged to go **to** town to-day, and as Ventry **is not** well, I asked Mr. Wiche if he would escort Felicia and myself to the Bishop's Bazaar this afternoon. I see now that it might cause gossip in the neighborhood : people make such absurd remarks. Besides, I fear it is scarcely kind to throw the poor man so frequently in the dear child's society. **Do you** think you could keep him amused in some way until we have left the house : we can pretend that there was some blunder and perhaps take

Mr. Van Huyster. . . . These things are difficult to explain."

" I think I understand," said Lady Mallinger : "of course, I will do anything to make myself useful. But I must at least change my gown : I heard him say that he liked **my** blue muslin !" She went **out** laughing so gaily, that Teresa, who was playing mournful music, left the piano and came down to her cousin.

" What is the joke ?" she asked.

Lady Twacorbie did not hesitate over her reply. She had made up her mind that Teresa was dying of love for the elegant Ventry and would therefore have no interest in the matrimonal schemes with regard to Sidney Wiche.

" Ventry has convinced me with regard to Van Huyster and Felicia," she said, at once. " Obstinacy is not one of my faults, and I am never deaf to reason. I have arranged everything in the most charming way : Lilian has agreed to distract **Mr.** Wiche's attention. Of course, dear, I would have asked you, but you are much too clever ! One can only trust a fool to carry out a plot of this kind with success. She is such a simpleton—just the silly creature to hoodwink a man of genius ! "

" Oh, this is too much ! " said Teresa. " I assure **you a** more accomplished actress **never** lived. **She is** far cleverer than either of us."

" Absurd ! Impossible ! " said **Lady** Twacorbie.

" There **is** nothing easier than the impossible—for Lady Mallinger. But **I am sure** that Sidney will **see** through her nonsense **at** once ; you must remember that he is my friend and I have known **him** for years : your plan will not succeed."

" But he admires her extremely," said Lady Twacorbie.

" Has he ever told **you so ?** "

" Of course not : it is **because he** has never said so, that I am certain of it. Men are dreadfully discreet, my dear Teresa. I only believe in what they do *not* say. But come, we **must** leave the coast clear, come ! "

Teresa followed **her** slowly.

V.

LADY MALLINGER reëntered the room a few moments later, in all her bravery of blue muslin, ribbons, and lace. She was cooing to the love-birds when Wiche came in. His acquaintance with Lady Mallinger had extended over some four years : from her point of view it might have been called a dinner-party friendship— that is to say, they could discuss people and subjects of the hour with a freedom which passes well enough for intimacy in the vagueness, bustle, and gigantic pettiness of a London season. But to Wiche their occasional meetings and interchange of ideas had meant much more; the man of letters is not a man of letters if he accepts life and the circumstances of life as they appear at first sight—it is the prime instinct of his nature to reject what *seems* and to clutch—or die in failing to clutch—things not as they are, but as his imagination would have them. To be brief, our friend had fallen in love with the idea of loving Lady Mallinger.

"Do I disturb you?" he said, and took a seat near her. She smiled at him and made a charming grimace at her pets.

"There is a bazaar at the Bishop's this afternoon," he continued, "and I believe I was expected to go, but as Van Huyster enjoys these things and I do not, I have asked Lady Twacorbie to take him in my stead. I hope she will not be offended, but

I really wanted to get a quiet hour with you."

Her heart jumped and she studied him with a new interest. There is one glory of the friend, **and another** glory **of** the possible lover. For the first time she discovered that he had a certain intensity, a masterful air, a look of determination—all of which she admired.

"We have so few opportunities to speak to each other," he said.

"**You** have changed since I **first** knew you," cried Lady Mallinger: "we were such good friends once, and now—when we meet—I hardly know how to describe it—there is a coldness, a restraint. I have feared that **you** did not like me. But I am saying too much."

"If I told you that there was indeed a reason for my restraint, would you care?"

She **put** her lips to the cage and

piped, apparently to the birds—
"Tell me the reason!"

"Have you never guessed it?
was I so hard to understand?"

"I could never understand any
man, but then a man never seems
able to explain himself, does he?"

"It may be that he dare not try,"
said Wiche.

"What could he fear?" she
asked; "can it be that men know
how unstable they are? I always
thought they could not, because
they never try to be firmer. And I
love firmness! Now we women
know only too well that we are
very weak, very foolish, very shal-
low, and we wonder what men can
see in us! We must be so tiresome!
such burdens! such unnecessary
evils! such tedious, provoking creatures! Some of us may have some
beauty; yet that soon goes, and
then there is nothing left of us but

a headache ! Oh, do not look surprised : I fear I am growing cynical. I am beginning to agree with many of your views **on** the soul, and death, and marriage, and things **of** that order ! "

"Ah ! never trust a man's opinion on any subject until he has been in love," said Wiche. "Love is the only thing which can make life **as** clear as noon-day."

"Then I suppose you **still** find it dark and perplexing ! **Dear** me ! how idly I talk. I meant to say—but would it be impertinent ? I was only thinking that a day, an hour, perhaps a few words might make all the difference in your ideas ! "

"If I told you," said Wiche, "that sleeping and waking I heard but one voice, saw but **one** face."

"Does it bore you ?" she asked ; "would you rather *not* see it ?"

"Each day," he continued, "it grows dearer to me, more beautiful, more—ah! if I waited until I were more eloquent I would never speak, never tell you my one hope, my one aim, my one ambition—above all things, beyond all things, before all things. Just—to gain you; to gain you—just that. I would not own it was impossible, I only saw you, loved you and waited. You passed me by, you hardly knew me. I was only one in a crowded world. A friend? Yes, when you remembered me. Was that often? Sometimes we talked together: once I wrapped you in your opera cloak, have you forgotten? I touched your cheek—it was an accident."

"As you say," murmured Lilian, "it only happened once."

"Another time you leant for a moment on my arm."

"That was a year ago."

"In March," he said, "it was a perfect night."

"Oh, no! it rained."

"A perfect night," he repeated, moving nearer, "and you never guessed **how much I loved you**— how much you were to me, how **much** I loved you! How beautiful, how very beautiful——" He kissed her.

Lady Mallinger started away in a sudden **panic.** "I did not mean to say so much," she said. "I did **not** mean—but hark!" She put her finger to her lips and flew across the room into a large chair with wide arms. These concealed her from Teresa Warcop who now **en**tered. She **was** evidently much agitated in spite of **her** quiet **man**ner. "I am so glad to find **you** alone," she said to Wiche, "**because** I must speak **to** you. But first let me say, **in justice to** myself, that I

am not a mischief-maker. If I ever
seem meddlesome it is only because
I am so interested in my friends
that I cannot remain silent when
speech would be of service to
them."

"You have too much heart," said
Wiche.

"I cannot bear to see a man deceived, trifled with, made a jest for
chattering vixens!" said Teresa,
passionately.

"The worst of it is that he rarely
shows gratitude if one endeavors to
enlighten him."

"A thankless task, I know," said
Teresa; "but if we only do our duty
for the sake of being thanked we are
miserable creatures. . . O Sidney!
never trust a woman! At least,
never trust blue eyes! Oh! when
I think of it, I lose all patience,
almost all charity. That such a
man should be duped by such a

7

woman ! Woman, did I say ? No,
a mere bundle of fire and frivolity ! ”

“ **How** much more **promising**
than mere flesh and blood,” exclaimed Wiche.

“ She made a bargain,” said Teresa, “a kind of wager—that she
would force you into a flirtation.
And she thinks she is succeeding :
she even began her machinations at
luncheon. I saw it all : her looks,
laughs, sighs. Oh, it was insup-
portable ! ”

“ Are you speaking **of** poor little
Felicia ? ” said Wiche.

“ Felicia ? ” said Teresa. “ Feli-
cia? When **I** speak of a creature
with neither heart, morals, mind,
nor beauty—a **heap** of lies, vanity
and affectation—I mean **Lady** Mallinger. ”

Wiche grew so pale that Teresa—
half with jealousy and half with
fright—grew even paler. She

held out both her trembling hands
and stumbled blindly towards
him.

"My heart has been with you,"
she stammered. "I feel it all, see
it all, know it all."

What she meant she hardly knew.
He neither looked nor uttered a
reply ; but, brushing past her with
a gesture hard to translate, walked
to the window. A stillness almost
like some grim and living presence
filled the room. Teresa remained
in her rigid attitude, staring, with
despairing tenderness, not at the
man, but at the place where he had
stood.

"A wager ! a bargain !" said
Wiche, at last. "I do not understand."

"Nor did I when I first heard
it," said Teresa. "I could scarcely
believe anything so odious, even of
her. And I have heard a good

many stories, too! But Charlotte explained the matter only too clearly. *Lilian was to distract you.* That was the expression : her own words." She paused a moment. Wiche **never** stirred, **but** kept one unchanging expression, which betrayed nothing save its unchangeableness. "Have I been wrong to tell you?" she went on; "have I been wrong? But friendship, my sense of justice, and you—the noblest man I **know,** the one above all others I—I respect."

"I do not understand you—or her," said Wiche, at last.

"**My** dear friend, men only understand the **kind** of woman who is more masculine than a man ! . . . But, Sidney, **are you** vexed with me? Have I been too zealous? You know, you surely believe I meant no malice? Yet I cannot **say that I feel** any kindness for

Lady Mallinger ; that would be impossible.   I despise her !"

"Is that necessary ? " said Wiche.

"Can I forgive her **conduct** towards yourself ? Not that she has succeeded in fooling you.   But the attempt—I cannot forgive the attempt.   What impudence ! what presumption ! "

"Ah, there you are unjust !   The feat was well within her power : I was only too willing to be fooled."

"Willing ! "   cried   Teresa. "Where is your spirit ?   How weak **a man is** after all !   What a mercy **that** she cannot hear you : it would make her even vainer than she is by nature."

"I fear we are growing too old and prosaic," said Wiche, bitterly ; "no wonder these young **people** try to rouse us."

"Sidney ! . . .   Do I seem so old ? "

"No one would guess your age," he said, without looking at her.

"Unfortunately, you know it!" said Teresa.   "Would you have forgiven *me*, if I had made such a bargain as this other woman? I think not."

Wiche did not hear the remark, or if he did, he made no reply.

She swallowed a sob and left the room.

VI.

ADY MALLINGER came forward half-crying, half-defiant.

"I cannot, I will not believe one word Teresa has said!" exclaimed Wiche. "She is the most honest soul in the world, but she makes mistakes."

"You would be wiser," said Lilian, slowly, "if you believed her."

"So you admit it," he said. "Do you think that Love is a plaything? a mood for a dull afternoon? a frame of mind to jump in and out of just for amusement? Is it noth-

ing to stake your life on another's,
to be faithful when they are faith-
less, strong when they are weak?
Is it so little to love like this? Do
you think it is so easy? Do you
think it brings much happiness?"

Until that hour, the devotion he
had felt for Lady Mallinger was
of that unreal kind which is only
dangerous so long as its object re-
mains an idea. It was to a great
extent theoretic, and based on the
dogmas of erotic poetry: in her
image he loved a dozen heroines—
not one woman. Now that he had
kissed her, however, and she had
shown herself sufficiently human
to rouse his anger, the whole rela-
tion changed. He no longer saw
her through the mist of sentimental
fancy; she was simply a pretty
woman who attracted him. He
felt vaguely that she might tempt
him to say and do much which he

would surely repent of. He repeated again, "Do you think such
love brings much happiness?"

"Ah! if you only knew me as
I know myself," murmured Lady
Mallinger. "All that Teresa said
of me was true—and yet, not true
enough. Everything about me was
falsehood and pretence, until—until
you seemed to believe in me. Do
you understand? Can you not see?
Are you so unforgiving, or—are you
only blind? Why are you so
silent?"

She held out her hand, which he
took half eagerly and half in dread:
her lightest touch seemed so much
more satisfying than all the wisdom
of the ancients.

"If I could only remain silent,"
said Wiche, passionately; "if I
could only keep you—only feel that
you were mine—mine—mine at all
risks! Yet no—you act too well.

I could never know how much I
was mistaken."

"Why should we refuse the
happiness this hour gives us, because some other hour might take
it away? In the meantime, there
can be no better thing than this.
No one before has ever cared
whether I was in jest or earnest,"
she faltered; "every other man
takes it for granted that I am heart-
less, brainless, and soulless in any
case. When I am serious, they say
I am in low spirits; when I am
sincere, they praise my hypocrisy.
So I take refuge in deceit, and I
succeed so well that now I have
deceived myself, and I no longer
know what I mean, what I want,
what I think, or what I am! To
judge me fairly, you should have
lived my life. My father was not
kind; at eighteen I married. The
world liked my husband: he ate

too much, drank too much, and made
too merry with **other** people's lives.
No one knows what I have suffered.
I have only found one thing which
outweighs disappointment—bitterness—all—all that is harsh, heavy
to bear, and terrible. That moment
—that one moment when you trusted
me. . . . It was so unexpected. I
had always liked you as a friend ; but
you seemed so far away, and **I**
thought you could only have contempt for me and my vain, hopeless
life. And the end of it all? Do
you suppose I never think of that?
Every night I say to myself, 'Another day has gone ; another day of
false hopes, false friends, false
loves, false hates, false griefs ! '
Think of it ! Not even a real grief :
my life, myself, all—all a sham ! "

"Help me to be as honest as you
are," said Wiche : "is there not
eternity before us ? the longest past

is but a second in comparison. See!" he said, kissing her, "we have forgotten it already!"

Men may still find oblivion in a kiss, but women of fashion are always—or nearly always—too self-conscious to forget the artificialities of life in the verities of passion.

"Forgotten already?" repeated Lady Mallinger, moving away from him, "I wish it were. Do not be angry with me, but I must be alone a little. There are so many things to think about—so many things. Give me half-an-hour."

"So much?" said her lover.

"Have we not eternity before us?" she replied.

Wiche laughed, kissed both her hands, and went out on to the Terrace : he found it almost as delightful to obey her whims as to worship her beauty. Only the strong-minded can know the extreme pleasure

of self-surrender.   Wiche's life had
been so hard, so serious, and, in a
sense, so wise until this too-en-
chanting present that he seized its
madness rather as a reward from
the gods than a curse.   He put all
thought of the future from his mind
—not because he feared it, but because it possessed no attraction for
him.   Lady Mallinger was an inex-
haustible delight : egoism, which in
any other woman seemed intoler-
able was, in her case, the most
charming thing in the world : self-
ishness, he argued, where the self
was so perfectly bewitching even
amounted to a duty : dull, tedious,
and unpleasant beings did well to
lose sight of themselves, but for
Lilian to forget herself would be
like a flower forgetting to bloom.

When Wiche had gone Lilian
paced the floor and mistook this
bodily exercise for deep thought.

She was brought to a standstill by finding herself face to face with Teresa, who, not being able to **quiet** her soul, had returned in the hope of seeing Wiche once more.

"You look depressed," **she said** to Lady Mallinger : "at luncheon you **were all** vivacity, epigram, and paradox.   If you had not told me I should never have suspected that you considered **it** your vocation **to** play the fool ! "

" Ah, **I am much wiser since our** conversation this morning," said Lady Mallinger.   "I am sure that the supreme happiness of a woman's life is to devote herself to the man who loves her : to be his friend, his ideal, his good angel !"

Teresa **smiled bitterly.** "And the supreme difficulty of a woman's life," she said, **"is to** find the man who desires such devotion, who *has* an ideal, who *wants* a good angel !

The best of men only ask us to be forever young and forever pretty : let your conscience go to the dogs but keep your freshness. Virtue never yet atoned for wrinkles ! "

"There I cannot agree with you," said Lady Mallinger. "I am sure that there is nothing so fascinating as sincerity ! It is so uncommon. I am going to be the most sincere woman in the world and I must begin by telling you that I was present just now during your conversation with Mr. Wiche."

"What conversation ? " said Teresa.

"Let us both be sincere, dear Miss Warcop ! I was sitting in that green chair when you mentioned my name, my first impulse was to rush forward : curiosity, however, intervened, and I remained in my corner. Perhaps this was wrong, but my position was diffi-

cult : to begin with, I agreed perfectly with every word you said :
you were. only too charitable. I
assured Mr. **Wiche** of this after-
wards, but he would not believe
me. When I told him that **I had**
indeed neither mind, morals, heart,
nor beauty, he looked so incredu-
lous, and was so deaf to all argu-
ment that I despair of convincing
him ! **Men** are so prejudiced.
What would you advise me **to**
do?"

"This sarcasm does not cut ! "

"Sarcasm ! " cried Lilian, "I
was never more candid, more
natural, more absolutely trans-
parent in my **life.** Why should I
dissemble when I have found that
you know me even better **than I**
know myself?"

"This innocent air may deceive
some infatuated man—for a time,"
said Teresa, "but I understand it

8

too well. How can you dare to
look so amiable when you know
that you hate me. . . . You
must hate me."

"Not at all : I think you are in-
discreet and perhaps too impulsive,
but, on the whole, I admire your
character : it has a stability, a dog-
gedness, a courage which mine
lacks. I would never have the
audacity, for instance, to discuss
your faults with Sir Ventry. He
would, I hope, be quite as blind
with regard to you as my future
husband is where I am concerned."

"Your future husband?" said
Teresa.

"Yes," said Lady Mallinger.
"Sidney was foolish enough to ask
me to be his wife—at least, in so
many words—and I was wise
enough to accept him ! If he will
only trust me and believe in me
always—if he will only see me—

not as I am, but as I should be—I am sure we shall be happy!"

"It is not hard to be good when you have **love and** sympathy and encouragement," said Teresa, warmly, "but to **be good** when not one soul cares whether you live or die, when your kindest thoughts, your least selfish acts, your dearest sacrifices are treated alike with insult, cruelty, and contempt—to be good then, that is the great achievement. Stand **alone,** be indifferent **to** smiles and frowns, keep your eyes steadily fixed on one unattainable ideal and condemn in yourself all that falls short of **it,** do that and **I** will call you happy! Defy slander, defy the malice of evil tongues and false hearts, **defy** even one **rule** of etiquette!"

"No woman has anything to fear except the truth," said Lady Mallinger, "**so long** as the truth will bear telling, she can laugh at lies. **They** may for a time work mischief, but only for a time."

"I, too, could have such a faith in the triumph of virtue if I had such a lover as Sidney!" said Teresa, "but live my life for a month and then tell me your philosophy!"

"You look cold," murmured Lilian, after a shiver and a slight pause.

"Cold! I am always cold : feel my hand."

Lady Mallinger held it to her own pink cheeks. "You make me like you," she said. "As a rule I do not care for women, and you are almost as spiteful as the rest. But there is something about you. . . . You believe me, when I say I like you?"

"Yet you have robbed **me of my** one friend," cried Teresa, "you— you **who** have so much already.

You are young and he thinks you
are beautiful : I shall soon be old
and I was always plain : many men
have loved my money, but no one
has ever loved *me*. In the Convent
—I was brought up in a Convent—
the sisters taught me how to live in
Heaven : they forgot I had to get
through the world first. My parents
are dead and now I have nothing in
this life except my wretched, hopeless interest in a man who has
never given me a thought. Perhaps I need not say that. He is
the only man I know who has not
asked me to marry him, so I think
he must like me a little. And he
comes to see me very often. But
you only care for him because he
flatters you, you are proud of him
because he is distinguished, but I
was proud of him when he was
poor and obscure, when every one
thought him an outcast, when it

was almost a crime in our miserable
little corner of society to be seen
even bowing to him. You do not
understand him as I do : you cannot help him as I could : you play
on all his weaknesses : every hour
he spends with you will be a step
backwards. Oh ! he is no hero in
my eyes, no passionless, faultless
machine, but a Man. . . . Go ! tell
him all I have said, laugh at me,
pity me, say ' Poor woman ! That
so plain and dull a creature should
fall in love ! How pathetic ! how
ridiculous ! ' "

Before Lilian could reply, Teresa
rushed out of the room. Lady
Mallinger rubbed her eyes : she,
too, had once loved like this and
she had been deceived. The mere
remembrance of Saville drove all
other thoughts from her mind : she
forgot Wiche, she forgot Teresa, she
forgot everything—the universe

contained but two beings—herself and Rookes. Fate brought **him to** her at that critical moment.

" I have been for a stroll with Sir Ventry," he began awkwardly. "I—I am wretched. **Are you still** angry?"

" I **do not** think we can have anything to say to each other, Saville," she said ; "the last words were spoken this **morning.** I could wish they had been kinder : I should **like to remember that we** parted, **at** least as friends. We were so much to each other once— once we thought it could never **come** to this. . . . Please leave **me."**

"No, I have been longing for a chance to speak **to you, now I** have found **it,** you must listen. I will not attempt to defend myself— I—— "

" You cannot : how could you?

You might perhaps **say** that you became desperate about your debts, and **so** — in a sort of madness — thought **to** marry Felicia **for** her money. You might say—ah, **a** thousand things, but they could make no difference. **It** is too late **to** think of them."

"Too late?" said Rookes. "How can **it be too** late when you are there and **I am** here." He knelt down by her side and, custom proving too strong for him, kissed her cheek. Custom was, perhaps, too strong for her also : at all events, she made **no** resistance. "You know my faults," he went on, "you could **never have** loved me for **my** perfection."

"I loved the man you might have been," she murmured, "not you at all." She glanced down and found **her hand** lying **in** his. "Not you at all," she repeated. "Be-

sides . . . it really is too late. I
— I have lost the right to listen to
you."

VII.

IN the meantime Wiche's half-hour had come to an end. The clock was chiming five when he appeared at the drawing-room window. Rookes sprang to his feet : Lady Mallinger affected to laugh.

"My cousin is teasing me," she said ; "he will not let me tell him that I am really a very serious woman. He—he does not believe in me as you do !" As she spoke she touched Wiche's arm as though to assert her ownership. Neither of the men spoke : a footman entered and announced that tea was served on the lawn.

"We must go then," said Lilian. She led the way, but when she turned, she found that only Wiche had followed her.

"It is as well," she said, in her prettiest manner ; " we are happier by ourselves !" This was no doubt charming, and it may have been true. Wiche, however, was no less troubled by the fact than the possibility. Both were distracting, for, at that moment, he wished to over-look her fascination and think only of what was certain. And the one thing certain was, in his judgment, her love for Rookes. This truth— like all truths — had flashed upon him like a message from his guardian angel.

"Do not look so grave," said Lady Mallinger ; "we have been serious the whole afternoon, and now I want to rest ! Do you like me in pink? Because I have the loveliest pink satin which I am dying to wear this evening."

"How old are you?" he said, suddenly.

"Oh ! My dear, dear Sidney ! One can see that you have never made love before ! How old am I? I forget : I was born so long ago. I must be at least twenty-two. Of course, I look even more, but then my life has been so unhappy. Now it will all be different, and perhaps I shall grow young again. You will be kind to me, will you not? And patient ? And you will not expect to find me very good, and very truthful, and very quiet all at once. You will give me time ? And you will not often be as cross as you are now, will you ? " At length she saw it was useless to ignore the demon who sat between them. "It was not my fault," she said, "it really was not my fault. I told Saville I had lost the right to listen to him. And now you are blaming me. **It is so hard** that I must always be made miserable—even when I have made up my mind to be contented. I have **tried my** very best," she added, "to be happy this afternoon!"

"Was it such an effort?" said Wiche.

"All—all **is an** effort," she answered, "except folly. **That** seems the only easy, natural, and pleasant thing in the world!"

"What do you call folly?"

"Everything I **want to do,** everything I want to say, everything I care for—that is what I call folly."

"My dear," said Wiche, " you are in love. And Rookes is the man!"

"Tut! How little you know

me ! I admit **that I am** greatly at-
tached to Saville—in spite of his
faults, but then I have known him
so long ! But in love with him—
never ! We are the dearest friends
possible, and quarrel incessantly—
but that is all ! ”

“Are you sure ? ” said Wiche,
“ are you sure that is all ? ”

She made no answer, but, **sooth-**
ing her lace which fluttered a little
in the breeze, hummed without
knowing it,

> “ Virtue how frail it is !
> Friendship how rare !
> **Love,** how it sells poor bliss
> For proud despair ! ”

“That,” said Wiche, gravely,
“is what Rookes was singing last
evening.”

“Pity me,” she murmured.

“Why ? ”

“I adore him ! ”

While we exist we can never es-
cape any stage of development ;
if our infancy be prematurely wise,
our years of discretion will have an
inappropriate childishness. Lilian
was living **life** backwards, and **her**
sudden moods of immaturity which
may have accounted for Rookes's
corresponding moods of fickleness,
filled Wiche with dismay. Passion
in these circumstances was impossible : affection ˙became angelic,
and sentiment lost **all** question of
sex.

"I adore Saville," she repeated,
and looked at Wiche with so be-
seeching an air, with such utter
helplessness and irresponsibility
that he wondered how he could
ever have mistaken her for **a**
woman. He still recognized her
grace and beauty, but it roused in
him the same kind **of** emotion a
man might feel **on** seeing the child

of one he had loved deeply and who was dead. It was a sorrowful task to trace the resemblance : to note the likeness in line, and delicate tones and expression : to say to himself, "Lilian's mouth had that curve, her eyes were that color, her throat was as white?"

"You must forget," he said, "you must forget—if you have not already forgotten—all that passed this afternoon. It was a great mistake."

*It was a **great** mistake.* Lady Mallinger brushed the echo of these words from her **ear** : she would not believe that they had ever been uttered. "This is what comes," she thought, " of telling a man the the truth : he flies !"

"You may have made a mistake," she replied, "but I have said nothing to you which I could ever wish to unsay. Saville told me this

morning that men may fall in love
dozens of times, but that each
experience is new. They can only
love once one way. This is true of
women also. And it all comes to
this : love is precisely the same
kind of emotion as religion. Oh, if
we would only be as patient with
human nature as God is ! Some
days we are more devout than
others : the saint who appeals to
you in one mood may repel you in
another : this month we devote ourselves to Our Lady, and another to
St. Paul ; some people, too, mistake
incense for dogma, and love of
music for love of virtue. But the
folly and sensuousness of creatures
like myself cannot touch the great
unalterable truths. I may never
know them as they are, but they
have been known. You will wonder
what I am trying to tell you. It is
hard to say : I believe I mean that
9

my adoration of Saville is not very
serious ! "

Wiche was a man who had learnt
what he knew of human nature
through self-discipline and not
through self-abandon. Knowing
therefore his own character and its
possibilities **so** well, he **was**
astonished to find that Lilian's was
so like—subject, of course, to certain feminine modifications. He
was acquainted with many men
who could give an accurate appraise-
ment of each and all their impulses,
thoughts, and emotions, who were
such skilled self-analysts that they
never by any chance confounded
their soul with their body, or their
conscience with either. **He** had
never met a woman, however, who
possessed this power even in a slight
and half-unconscious degree ; he
looked at Lilian and felt that while
she had cured him of his fit of love,

she had never seemed so deeply interesting as a fellow-creature.

"My dear," he said, "you must surely see that we should be wretched if we married."

"Why?" said Lilian, "it would be such a comfort to me to have some one I could really trust and believe in; some one who would help me to be serious; to know one being at least who was not led away by all manner of idle fancies!"

The irony of the situation would have been ludicrous if it had not been so heart-breaking.

"Do not imagine that I am that one being," said Wiche, hastily. "God knows I am flimsy enough. And I am afraid it is always disastrous to pin one's faith to a mere mortal. Even the best of us are miserably imperfect as rocks of defence; you see we are flesh-and-blood, we are not granite."

"Treat me as though I had a mind, Sidney," she said, " and I will follow you to the ends of the earth ! "

"I do not think," he stammered, "we could ever be happy together."

"You mean," said Lady Mallinger, "that you do not care for me in the way you thought."

"I will always be your friend," he said, firmly, " but——" Her sense of what was just and meet told her that it only remained now to call her soul into her eyes, gaze mournfully at Wiche, and leave him. Saville after all loved her the best.

Women like Lady Mallinger have to die young in order to be understood : then—and then not always —some onlooker more discerning than the others will see in the cold body some trace of a fiery spirit too ardent and too restless for mortality.

Alas! poor soul. Seeking the highest, best, most beautiful, and purest —and finding a Saville Rookes.

The modern is always an unwilling slave to sentiment : if he find himself captivated by a romantic love or a sublime ideal he accepts his state in the shamefaced and hopeless certainty that his common-sense will one day come to the rescue. He cannot believe that what he takes for beauty will always be so fair, or that what seems good for the moment could be inspiring forever. Satisfaction only makes him restless : he sighs for happiness and, having found it, sighs lest, after all, it should only be a shadow cast by his own desires. Wiche therefore suffered his disappointment with smiling patience and with something even of relief; once he had doubted that all was vanity, had suspected that life yet held

much that was precious and desirable, that love was an immortal
fact, and endured. He felt now that
he need struggle no longer against
despair, and, abandoning himself to
the intense pleasures of profound
melancholy, became agreeably tired
of existence. To his unspeakable
resentment, however, one shining
thought pierced the blackness of his
thoughts. Teresa still remained.
But she had never been his ideal.
Teresa was Teresa—a vivid, distinct
personality, a being whom no
amount of romantic disguise could
make seem other than she was, and
who was incomparable, not because
of her singular merits, but because
no one else had the same faults.

VIII.

SIR VENTRY COXE had been educated in the belief that his cousin Teresa loved him madly. When he married Lady Susan Hoppe-Gardner, a chorus went up from all the members of his family. "What on earth will poor Teresa do?" She was present at the wedding, nevertheless, and seemed in the best possible spirits : the relations looked wise and murmured that it was impossible for the unhappy girl to deceive *them*. Ventry was particularly kind to her; he clasped her hand warmly when he started on his honeymoon and thanked **her** again and again with tears in his eyes for her magnificent gift in the shape of **a diamond necklace for his** bride : every one said **it** was too touching for words, several ladies declared that Teresa grew as **white as a** sheet and would have swooned if Lord Twacorbie, with his ready tact, had not led her to the air.

A few years passed ; Miss Warcop refused all offers ; Lady Susan died. This, all the relations said, **was Fate.** Sir Ventry, remembering Teresa's rent-roll, thought so too. He decided to make her his wife when a decent period of mourning had elapsed ; there was no hurry, she was there, ready, waiting, and willing, when he wanted her.

The day at last dawned when it seemed convenient to address her on the subject : he met her in the hall as she left the drawing-room

after her scene with Lady Mallinger.
She was greatly embarrassed, a fact
which he easily attributed to her
sudden encounter with **himself**.
Smiling magnanimously, he waited
until she had regained her **com-
posure**.

"Shall we go into the garden?"
he suggested.

No, she was feeling rather tired;
she had a slight headache; he would
find her a very **dull** companion.

"*Do* come," he said, **in** his most
persuasive manner.

Teresa, who was always amused
at his conceit, and who had a motherly, pitying affection for the weaknesses which did **duty** for his character, yielded the point and followed
him. **He** began **to** talk of former
days: he reminded her of his five-
and-twentieth birthday, when she
gave him a hunter and wore a black
cloak lined with scarlet.

"You look awfully well in scarlet," he observed.   She blushed :
scarlet was Wiche's favorite color.
Sir Ventry, however, took the blush
to himself.

"I always admired you, you
know," he said; "there is not a
woman in the family who has got
such a complexion, and your eye-
lashes are so long."

"It is very nice of you to say so,"
said Teresa :   "I, myself, do not
think they are bad.   Once or twice
I have thought I looked quite decent !"

He glanced at her sideways.   Was
she really so plain as all the women
made out?

"I am awfully fond of you," he
said suddenly.

Teresa was by no means dense.
"My dear Ventry," she said, with
rather a nipping air, "let us talk
like reasonable beings."

"I am quite serious," he replied. "Will you marry me, Teresa?"

"Certainly not. You must be mad."

"What!"

"You must be mad. And think yourself very lucky that I forgive you for making such an insulting suggestion." Trembling with anger she left him. He looked up to see whether the Heavens were falling.

IX.

TERESA sat alone in the drawing-room before dinner that evening. The lamps were lit and their hazy light fell on the orange velvet draperies, the vases of blue Sevres, the Chinese embroideries on scarlet satin, the copper bowls, the tiger skins and the Indian shawls. Teresa loved colour, gorgeous sunsets, the blare of trumpets, loud music—all that could send some note of the tremendous into the undramatic tragedy of her existence. To-night she wore a gown of silver brocade: lace concealed her neck, and long sleeves her arms, but neither brocade nor lace could hide the slight, almost angular figure of their wearer. She held a book of devotions in her lap, the leaves of which **she** turned at random, but her glance fell now on the clock, and now on the mirror— rarely on the volume and its grotesque old woodcuts of saints and ecstatic virgins. At last the sound of footsteps in the corridor without, and the opening of **a** door, marred the disquieting repose **of** her vigil. She let fall the book of prayers : the little crash it made on striking **the floor and** the rustle of her silk petticoat drowned the words of greeting **which she** addressed **to** Wiche, who now entered.

He chose a chair near hers, but she, half-unconsciously, shrank back. **He** was too engrossed in his own thoughts, however, to notice the movement.

"I fear I seemed most ungrate-
ful this afternoon," he said, "but I
felt quite sure that you would one
day understand **Lady** Mallinger,
and know, **as** I do, the real woman.
Perhaps I should say the real child."

"When I spoke," said Teresa, in
a low voice, "I did not know that
you loved her. And she has
charmed **away my** prejudice since
then. I will frankly admit that I
did not wish to discover anything
bewitching either in her face or in
her manner. I **only** wanted to
have the right to detest her with a
clear conscience !"

"Yet, in spite of all this, she conquered you?"

"She conquered me," repeated
Teresa, "but let me say one thing
—she is too romantic : she lives by
moonlight."

Wiche laughed. "She has seen
a great **deal** of the world," he said,

"and I have often been struck by her extraordinary, almost terrible common-sense. She may have a certain amount of sentimentalism in her brain, but at heart she is cold and critical. This ache to be amused, this longing to hear music in the air, to see beauty on all sides, to find life one ever-new, yet ever-abiding pleasure, these are the fierce, never-gratified desires of those who love only themselves. But to him who loves others—even one other" —he found himself looking into Teresa's eyes—"even one other— the commonest things seem rare, the blackest shadows have a radiance indescribable, and the harshest notes are heavenly melodies : disappointment, bitterness, and desolation have no part in his existence !"

"These exalted moods are brief— terribly brief," said Teresa, "and

they show us just enough of our
lost divinity to make us ever more
wretched as mere mortals and children of Adam.   It is the day after,
the days after, the weeks, months,
years after, when we can only remember that once we were happy for
half-an-hour!"   She seemed to have
forgotten Wiche's presence, and he
felt that she was thinking of something in her own experience in which
he bore no part.   It was certain that
she could have no knowledge of his
love-adventure with Lady Mallinger,
and he could not make up his mind
to tell her the news just then.

"I wonder," he said, abruptly,
"I have often wondered why you
are the only one in the world I can
talk to without the dread of saying
either more or less than I mean."

"I will **tell you** why," she answered: "I could never misunder-
stand you, Sidney, because I love

you." Although she was a woman
in whom the coquette was, at all
events, slumbering, her primmest,
least emotional manner had the
mysterious charm of those things
which we note unmoved and remember with passionate interest.
She made her declaration of love so
quietly that Wiche saw neither its
oddness, nor, indeed, its full mean-
ing : he colored a little, however,
at the sense her words might have
conveyed.

"Do not think I am choosing
phrases at random," she went on,
"I meant what I said. There is only
one thing in my life which I can be
grateful for—that is my love **for**
yourself. Many people would think
it very unwomanly on my part to
tell you this ; I am only proud **to**
know that I am capable of loving
any one. All affection seems to
have been laughed out of the

10

world : when it is not ridiculous, it
is thought hysterical. **To me it re-**
mains and always must remain, the
greatest—the only perfect gift—that
God has given us. So I have told
you." Her lips trembled a little as
she added, "I suppose, too, you
have heard it already from Lady
Mallinger ? "

"What could I hear from Lady
Mallinger," he asked, growing more
and more bewildered. Teresa's expression was so frigid though her
words were so kind. "I am sure
we are talking at cross-purposes."

"Do you mean to say," she
stammered, "that she never told
you all—all I said to her this afternoon ? "

"She has never uttered **your**
name."

Teresa hid her face in her hands
and forced back her tears. She had
needlessly betrayed her secret.

" I will explain," she said, at last. " Lady Mallinger told me this afternoon that she was going to marry you : we had some words and I—I confessed quite plainly what I—I said just now. And I thought **she** would surely repeat it—so—in order to avoid any misapprehension —I decided to let you hear it from me also. It needed courage, but now all my courage has gone—I had only enough for that. **It** wanted so much. **Do** not say a word ; please go. "

"Lady Mallinger is not going to marry me," he said, quietly.

He touched Teresa's hand, and conquered his impulse **to** kiss **it :** that was not the moment, nor indeed could he imagine a time when it might be the moment. **She** seemed to stand **in** an enchanted circle. Suddenly, he saw that she was crying. This touch of weakness seemed to supply the one thing he had always missed in her character. Teresa had, as a rule, a self-command which was almost forbidding — even her occasional indiscretions had something well-considered and reasonable. She lacked that inconsequence, that capriciousness, that delicious non-sense which most men and all strong natures find so alluring and adorable. To see her weeping, therefore, was to behold a new creature. Wiche was uncertain how to reply, when she herself, brushing the tears from her cheeks, asked him a question.

"Why?" she said, "why are you not going to marry Lady Mallinger?"

"I want to tell you about that," he said. "I am afraid that there is not time to tell the whole story now. But Lady Mallinger dis-covered that she had made a mistake, she loved some one else, and I — I have been such a fool, Teresa, such a fool! I do not know whether I love you or not. I only know that I hate my life when you are not near me!" This truth, which had been sleeping so long, woke at the first whisper of its name: he realized how pitiably little would remain to him if Teresa were taken from his memory: it was her very oneness with his own mind which had made him overlook her: when he imagined he was thinking of himself he was thinking of Teresa also.

"I only know," he said once more, "that I hate my life when you are not near me!"

She could have wished that he had expressed himself with less egoism; if he cared for her at all it was because she was necessary to his peace of soul: at least, so it sounded. But she was a woman who found her happiness in giving and loving : she made no demands ; she looked neither for gratitude, **nor** homage, nor appreciation ; she **only** asked the right to give and to love. So she gave Wiche her hand ; her heart had been his from the beginning.

"Without you," she said, "I have no life to hate ! "

This may have been weak, but Teresa was **not** strong-minded. And perhaps it is as well for those **of us** who are proud and self-reliant **that** just such simple, undignified, and affectionate creatures are to be found here and there. They may speak for **us on** Judgment Day, which will be the longest, darkest, and coldest, this world has seen.

X.

"ARDEN LODGE,

"NEAR WENSLEY,

"MERTFORD.

"MY DEAR HAROLD,—I am so annoyed and disgusted that I can scarcely hold my pen. Wiche has proposed to *Teresa*, and has been accepted. What could be more outrageous than such conduct? As for Teresa, you know I always thought her dreadfully sly. How any woman could prefer Wiche to Ventry! But there, what on earth

151

does Wiche see in Teresa? Van
Huyster told me in the course of
conversation at dinner that he is
engaged to some American person
in Paris, and that he hopes to per-
suade her to marry him on the
Fourth of July. We must really be
more careful in future about whom
we invite to the house. Lilian and
Rookes are flirting in the most unexpected manner. I thought they
could not *bear* each other. *Nothing*
however, would astonish me in that
direction after the surprises of this
day. I believe that I am the only
sane person in the house. Thank
goodness, they all go to-morrow.
I long for rest. Felicia seems hysterical; I never knew a girl of
seventeen with so many nerves.
She must go on with that steel tonic
and take fencing lessons.

"Your affectionate wife.

"CHARLOTTE TWACORBIE.

" P.S.—Spalding has just been in to say that he and Danby wish to get married this day month ! What could be more tiresome ? I begged him to reconsider it, **but he** said it was too late. **He** had **made** up his mind.

"**P.S.** No. 2.—Ventry has given **me to** understand that he proposed to Teresa this afternoon, and **that** she seemed quite annoyed. **He is** furious, **and** blames ME. I dare not tell him about Wiche."

TO

WALTER SPINDLER.

AH, not for me—to learn the truth by
  dreaming,
To hear the cries of earth in melody,
To know 'tis night but when the stars are
  gleaming,—
      Ah, not for me.

Music of form and colour's mystery,
The joy of fashioning in fairest seeming
Life's dullest clay and Winter's barest tree;

To count the years as moments—only
  deeming
That truly Time which makes thy Art to
  thee
The one thing needful and the all-redeem-
  ing,—
      Ah, not for me!

September 23, 1893.

155

EPILOGUE.

*Spoken by a Daughter of Eve, who is weeping,
and an Angel, who looks out of fashion.*

THE ANGEL.

This is only Sorrow
For To-Day.
Life begins To-Morrow !

A DAUGHTER OF EVE.

So they say.

THE ANGEL.

Life with love and laughter
Gay and free—
Yet no heartache after.

A DAUGHTER OF EVE.

Can it be?

THE ANGEL.

Life with work that reaches
To the sky ;

157

Life that never teaches
How to die.
Life that is eternal,
Ever young,
Ever bright and vernal
Just begun!

A Daughter of Eve.

Will To-Morrow ever dawn?
Shall we wake that golden morn
But to see
All the treasures gained by tears,
All the faith that's **won** by fears—
Vanity?

The Angel.

Doubter, look behind thee
In the **past,**
All the **dreams that pleased thee**
Did one last?
Is a wish remaining
From thy youth?
This thou art retaining
If 'twas truth.
Mortal passions sicken,
Fade away—
Love alone can **quicken**
Earthly clay.
Faith, and all endeavour
That is pure,
Hope, and Love, for ever
These endure.

All things else are folly
To the wise,—
Quit thy melancholy
And thy sighs !

.

www.ingramcontent.com/pod-product-compliance
Lightning Source LLC
Chambersburg PA
CBHW031156050726
47495CB00019B/2251